SUZ HUGHES

Curious Fox

For Margaret and Tony

First published in 2016 by Curious Fox,
an imprint of Capstone Global Library Limited
264 Banbury Road, Oxford, OX2 7DY
Registered company number: 6695582
www.curious-fox.com

Copyright © Suz Hughes
The author's moral rights are hereby asserted.
Illustrations by Suz Hughes

All characters in this publication are fictitious and
any resemblance to real persons, living or dead,
is purely coincidental.

ISBN: 978-1-78202-515-3 (paperback)

20 19 18 17 16
10 9 8 7 6 5 4 3 2 1

A CIP catalogue for this book is available from the British Library.

Designer: Lori Bye

Printed and bound in China.

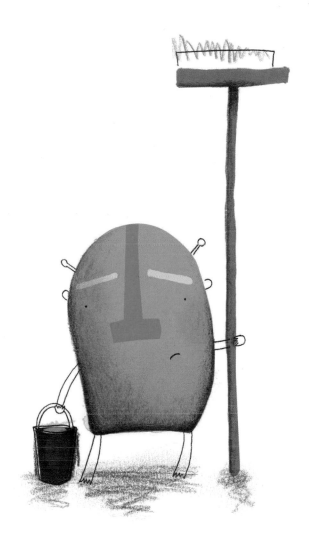

There once was a tiny alien with a very BIG job.

Alien was a star shiner. Every night, he kept the stars shining. Alien took his job VERY seriously — maybe a bit too seriously.

Alien never took time off to do anything fun, and he didn't have any friends.

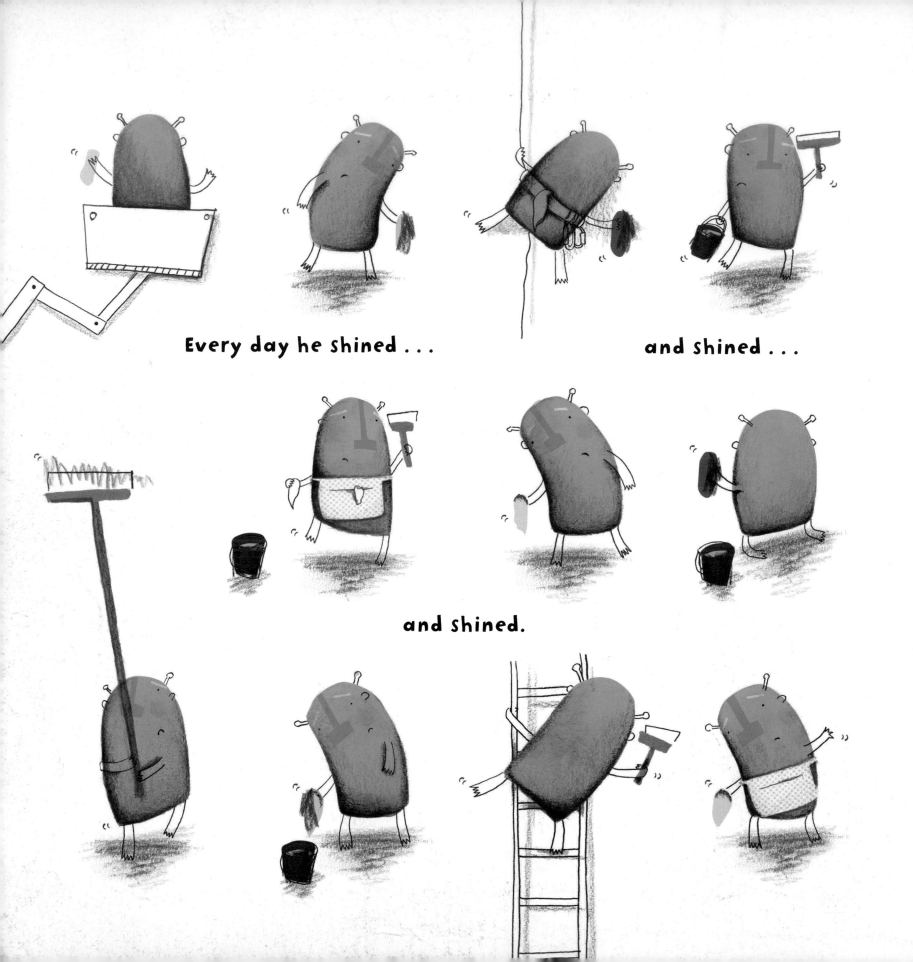

Every day he shined . . . and shined . . .

and shined.

Shining is all he did! But one night,
something disastrous happened . . .

The stars went out!

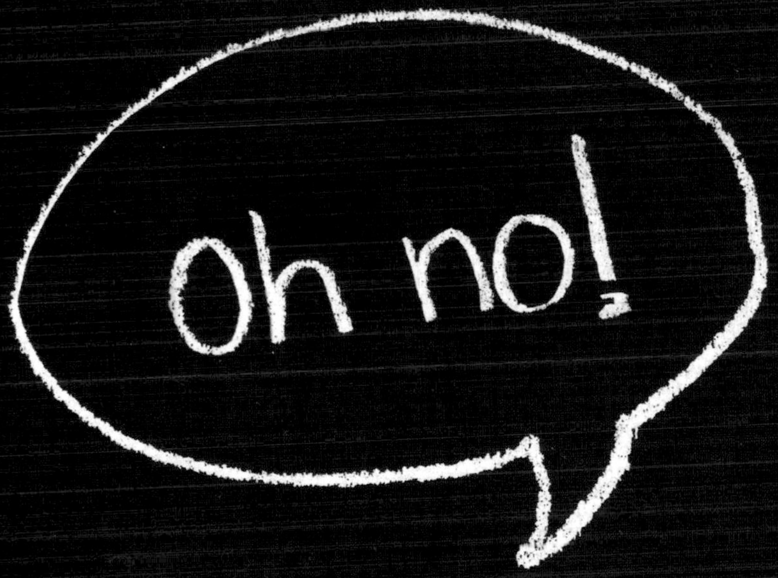
Oh no!

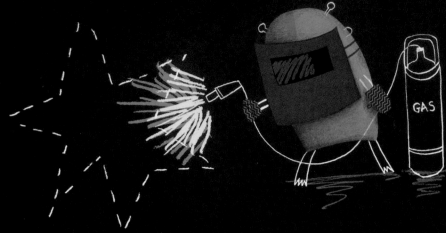

"Did I shine the stars too much?"
Alien wondered.

He tried everything to fix the
problem, but nothing worked.

Alien was desperate, so he called the Star Helpline.
They told him he needed a magic varnish, but the
varnish was only sold on a faraway planet called Earth.

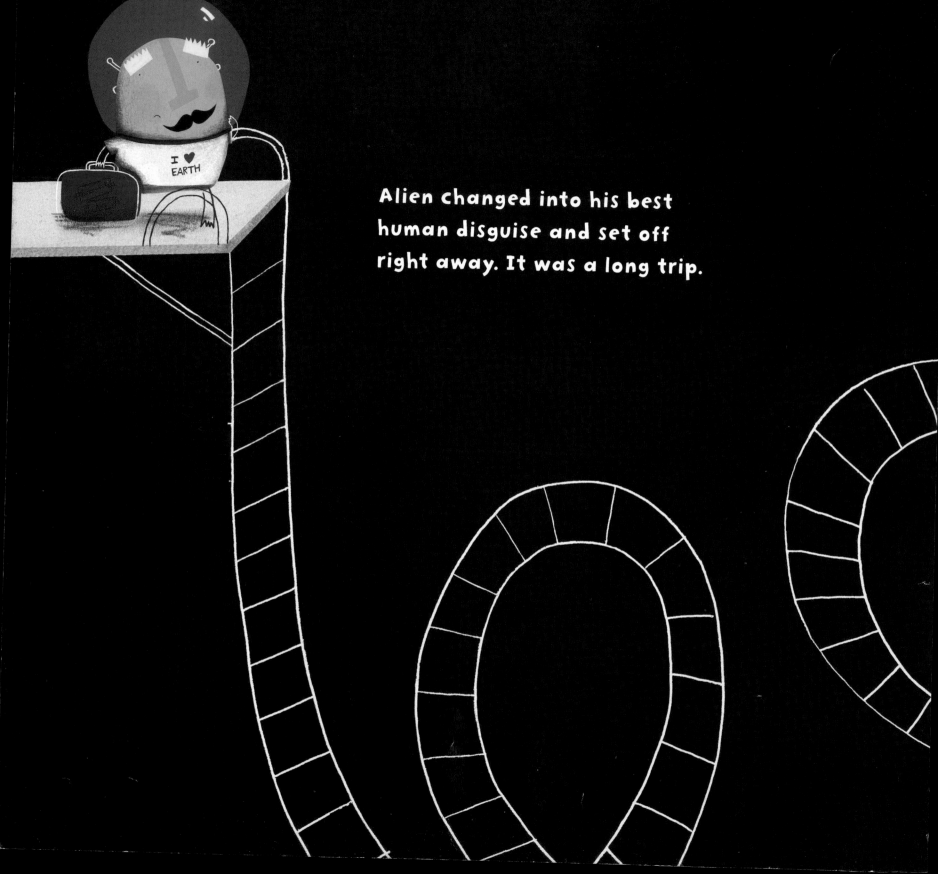

Alien changed into his best human disguise and set off right away. It was a long trip.

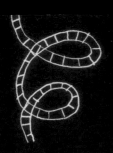

When Alien finally arrived on Earth,
he learned something interesting.
On Earth, aliens float!

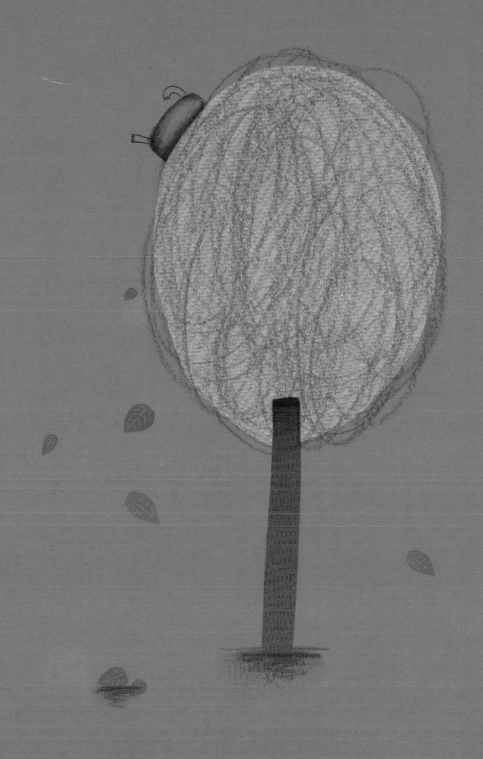

Alien hadn't planned for this, and he got
himself into a bit of a tangle.

Alien kept yelling and finally got the attention of a young boy and his dog.

"Hello. Can you help me, please?" Alien asked.

"Sure," the boy replied.

Alien's moustache was itchy, so he ripped it off.

"I'm Alien," he said.

"I'm George," the boy replied, letting the balloon go and kindly tying Alien to the string so he wouldn't float away. "What brings you to Earth?"

Alien explained the situation, feeling sadder by the minute.

George listened carefully. When Alien
finished telling him about the problem,
George said, "We can fix this! Come on.
Let's go to the hardware shop."

Alien didn't know what a hardware shop
was, but he was willing to try anything.

At the hardware shop, George knew
exactly where to find the magic star
varnish. They wasted no time stocking up.

"Do you want to play with me for a while?"
George asked.

Alien wasn't sure. He needed to get the stars
back on, but George had been so helpful.

"Okay," Alien said.

Alien couldn't believe how wonderful it was to play. He had never had so much fun!

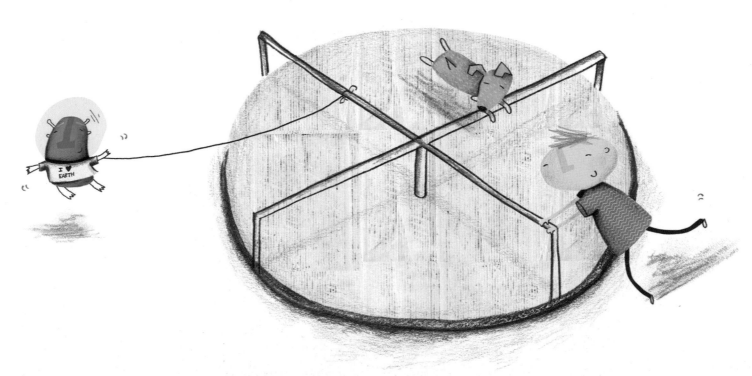

They
giggled
and
giggled
and
giggled.

Alien felt very strange. His body felt light, and he couldn't stop smiling. He was happy!

Then something extraordinary happened . . .

. . . the stars turned on!

"How did you do that?" George asked.

"I didn't," said Alien. "You did! You made me happy! I didn't need magic star varnish after all. I just needed a friend."

"Let's promise to stay friends forever," George said. "That way, the stars will never go out again."

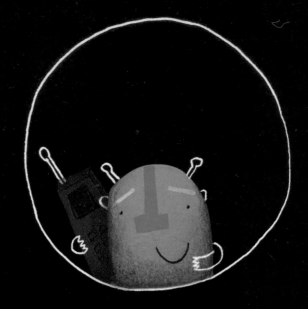

And together, they're still keeping that promise.